The Blue Box

The Blue Box

Flash Fiction & Poetry

Ron Carlson

 Red Hen Press | *Pasadena, CA*

Book design, layout, and cover by Michelle Olaya-Marquez

Library of Congress Cataloging-in-Publication Data
Carlson, Ron, author.
  The blue box / Ron Carlson.
     pages cm
  ISBN 978-1-59709-275-3 (paperback)
  I. Title.
  PS3553.A733B58 2014
  813'.54—dc23

                              2014019060

The National Endowment for the Arts, the Los Angeles County
Arts Commission, the Los Angeles Department of Cultural Affairs,
the Pasadena Arts & Culture Commission and the City of Pasadena
Cultural Affairs Division, and Sony Pictures Entertainment par-
tially support Red Hen Press.

First Edition
Published by Red Hen Press
www.redhen.org

Acknowledgments

Several of these stories and poems have appeared in the following publications:

DASH Literary Journal, "Walk-bridge" as "Rockbridge"; *Emeritus Voices*, "In Jeddah"; *Fire on the Beach*, "Horror Story at Lonely Lake"; *Hayden's Ferry Review*, "My True Style Guide"; *McSweeney's*, "You Must Intercept the Blue Box before It Gets to the City"; *Meridian*, "My Soldiers"; *Narrative 4*, "How to Be a Man"; *PML*, "Who Will Withstand the Test of Time?"; *Redivider*, "The Captain's Daughter"; *Slice*, "Party at the Beach Party House"; *SmokeLong Quarterly*, "How Things Have Actually Changed Since We Did Secede from the United States"; and *Tin House*, "Recommendation for Gordon Lee Bunson."

For Griffin and Atticus

Contents

I

II

"I knocked out your pop with gas bombs and I carried him to New York in chains, and I've regretted it ever since."

—Carl Denham in *Son of Kong*

The Blue Box

I

You Must Intercept the Blue Box before It Gets to the City

Get that box! It must not get to the city; everybody knows that. It must be stopped from getting to the city. Go after the box and make sure it does not reach the city. Act quickly and intercept the box before it arrives in the city. Go to the shipping terminal and run through the big warehouse, past the conveyor belts carrying all the packages and boxes and cardboard tubes full of maps. Run! If you see a blue box, check it out. Some will be too small, some too big. Don't be fooled by the other blue boxes. When you see it dumped into the delivery truck, note the truck's number, like if it is seventeen or ninety, some number and pursue that truck. I guess you'll use a motorcycle. Just jump on a motorcycle and chase that truck. The box! Drive ahead of the truck and signal the driver to stop. When you check the back of the truck, all the boxes will be blue! This is bad, and all you can do is turn around and watch the driver run away with one blue box! That is the box you must stop from getting to the city. Chase him on foot, even if he climbs onto the roof of that building. Go up the rain gutter, climbing the way you were trained in your other life, where you were lonely, strong, and sad, and run across the rooftops. When he slips down the Italian tile roof and falls three stories to the ground, quickly climb down the wall using your techniques. Yes, he's dead! Or is he? He could be faking. Some guys in this spot fake it and lie there. But where is the box? Could it be magnetized to the back wall of the dumpster in the alley by his body? Look there. No, because the box is not magnetic! Quick. Think. How do you stop the blue box from getting to the city? Everyone you love lives in the city. You only love a few people, say three or four, depending. You admire your nephew, he's in the top rank at his institute, but you don't love him. He's annoying and smug and expresses so many things in decimals. I like this coffee about six point two, he says. So smug. But still, he lives in the city. And your lost love lives in the city, whom you still love from afar with a chaste benevolence, and your sister lives in the city, mother of your know-it-all nephew who you like about four point four, and your major love interest lives in the city, and she is interesting. She's been there for you so many times, and there and there. You want to be there for her. She teaches children every day at a school in the city, dozens of children who are ardent about their studies and singing in music class and astronomy with Mr. Myers and soccer when they play the intramural tournament on the grassy field, the Gray versus the Red and the Green versus the Orange because Mr. Demaray in his checkered sweater will let the games go until almost dark, and it all feels like part of a complicated legend. Some nights in the fall, the children run and call and kick the ball until the final whistle blows and they walk back to the yellow windows of the school, their breath plumes in the chilly October air.

Warm, Buttered, Cinnamon Toast Killed Cranky Bear

That is the whole story! Why would there be anything more? What exactly is it you don't get about what happened to Cranky Bear? He was Cranky Bear, and then the cinnamon toast killed him, the end! The end! Stop looking for what else because you're too stupid to see what happened to Cranky Bear! He was cranky! Everybody says, he was so cranky! What are you, the Cranky Bear? This was a common remark. It wasn't even a question. How rude is that? Somebody comes in the kitchen only to be met with a crude new name: Cranky Bear! What about something a little more understanding, such as Tired Bear or Hungry Bear, even Tired Hungry Bear. No! That's not going to happen! It's Cranky Bear. And what happened? The toast popped up. He didn't know it was cinnamon toast, and he went at it with a butter knife and saw the butter melting in the toast and he took a few bites, ate some of the cinnamon toast with the warm butter and that was about it. The end, okay! Get it. Warm, buttered, cinnamon toast killed Cranky Bear!

Who Will Withstand the Test of Time?

First of all, I was late for the
Test of Time because I had read the bulletin
wrong and I went to McDougal Hall and
it was clear over in the Hayes Auditorium
where they have the physics lectures, and
then when the monitors distributed the Test
of Time I saw that I was in my underwear
and not my good ones. In the actual Test of
Time my pencil kept breaking, I mean more
than once, and I needed an eraser very bad-
ly. It was important that I erase some of my
answers completely and cleanly because I
knew they were wrong, but I also knew that
my eraser was lost somewhere and now outside the windows of the Hayes Auditorium
I could see it raining from the dark skies.
My answers on the Test of Time were horrid
and embarrassing and slightly smudged so I
stood up and explained to the monitor that
I needed to go and get my eraser and that
explanation took an hour blah blah blah in
my old underwear and I lied to her telling
her the eraser was home in my desk drawer
when I knew it was really gone or at least
far away and I also knew as soon as I went
outside and started running barefoot in the
rain I would never ever return to the Test
of Time

but as I pushed the heavy door of
the Hayes Auditorium open there you were
with my favorite shirt and my blue jeans
and slippers and when I was dressed and I
buttoned the last button on that soft green
shirt you turned me around and pushed the
eraser into my pocket.

Sate

Hillyard loved to say the word "sate." He was sixteen and he'd dialed it up accidentally one day and saw his father flinch, and so it was now mandatory in every paragraph. At dinner, he would compliment his mother on the meal and then announce to the table, his mother, his father, and Hildy, his sister, who was a year older, "I'm about sated by this great meal. No, in fact I am sated. I've been sated here. What about you? I am absolutely sated."

Hildy wasn't used to being around her brother when he spoke in sentences; it seemed to her he had been a grub for years, and now he was talking, and she regarded him most with simple curiosity wondering if he even was the same creature. "I can't tell which element sated me," Hillyard went on. "The asparagus was a wonder, but I don't think it led the way. I think the mashed potatoes certainly sated me."

He loved to take his time turning the corners in his sentences and his father who taught history at the high school knew to listen for *absolutely* and *certainly* and *actually.* "So many people are sated on potatoes, but in my case, I think it was actually the roast that sated me completely over the top." His father thought of tipping Hillyard off to the word *indubitably.*

"Sated like this," Hillyard went on, "I think I'll excuse myself and access the television. So good to see you all." And he would stand slowly and put a hand on the top of his non-existent stomach. Pushing his chair back, he added, "It's a documentary on cork, the history of cork." He was a kid who never rushed anywhere and it was a little nervous-making the way he stood behind his chair waiting for someone to say something about cork. Finally he lifted both hands, fingers spread and backed from the room. If he goes on the stage, his father thought, we'll all be able to retire.

Party at the Beach Party House

We were all living in the beach party house like eight or nine of us. Ten. All guys and we were wearing bathing suits all the time talking in groups of two or three. Four. We were having fun and having parties every afternoon and every night. We sat on the porch of the beach party house and talked, saying things like, "Oh Buzz, this is too much," and "Get ready for the party, boys!" The place was really more of a shack; okay, it was a shack. We always had a bonfire at the parties, and somebody sang with a guitar. Some songs were funny folk songs and some were slow love songs. When someone sang, everybody, all the guys, listened. We would lean against something and listen to the songs at the parties. When someone finished singing, we would applaud and talk to each other and take the hand of the girl who was near us. The girls wore two piece bathing suits which were yellow and red and blue. Sometimes it was hard to tell who was with whom, but we carried on at the beach party shack. The girls all evidently lived at home. They did not live in a beach party shack or any shack at all; we wouldn't associate with girls from shacks. When it grew late at night, the girls left to go home. Probably. No girls stayed at the Beach Party House overnight. That would have been too weird, and these were pretty girls. They looked too old for high school, but they were in high school. "Goodbye goodnight," we called, and the girls all ran away in their bathing suits. It was too much. We knew it would all happen again tomorrow. We sat in the shack late at night, ten young men. With the girls gone, we unlocked the secret door and went into the wooden steps into the basement and continued our work on our weapons.

The Moon

A walk in the night. And here comes the moon.
So beautiful and always up in the sky. Okay, we get it.
Oh beautiful moon up in the sky. In the night so beautiful
Etcetera infinity double beautiful beautiful and so on
Orbiting the earth while I'm trying to walk here,
Oh beautiful moon, beauty beauty, glowing disk and the like
Orbiting orbiting, circling the earth like a stalker,
We get it, we see you, now just let it go. I need a walk
And I need the dark, frankly, you glowing gewgaw,
Moon moon moon moon moon.

The Pitcher Sees the Coach Approach

Regardless of when it occurs, early in the game as
they say or in the late innings, you hate to see her come to
the dugout steps and put her hand on the rail there and start
to come onto the field. Maybe you've walked a couple
three batters in a row, throwing wild pitches all around the
clock, or you've given up back to back doubles or triples or
singles and a homerun hit so far out of the stadium it filled
the crowd with reverence and fear, even then when you're
throwing like a secret agent for the other team, you hate to
see her coming your way. She's someone, actually, you
really enjoy seeing on all other occasions, and there have
been times when you've seen her or she's approached you
or you her, and it has lit up your day, in fact, you like her
plenty truth be told, and you've got your reasons for that
affection and her personal beauty is only a part of it. She's
fair and easy to talk to and she's an optimist and reads
books and has brushed things off your shoulder without
making a face or a fuss and she drinks a glass of water with
both hands, something that just touches your heart. But
now, as she walks across the green green grass of foul
territory and then steps over the base path into the infield, it
doesn't feel quite so wonderful. She looks good, as always,
but whenever you meet like this on the mound in front of
sixty thousand people who are watching your exchange, it
isn't a pleasurable experience. It's so much better when you
have a late supper on the terrace at the Golden Glove or in
one of the Big Booths in the back of Fungoland and there is
no one around but the waiter and you watch her drink her
water holding the glass with both hands and you explain the

Infield Fly Rule to her so clearly that she almost cries and you set out your hopes for your future as a right hander in this league and you tell her something very personal and it is the feeling that floods your chest when you fire a rising fastball past the batter and the umpire calls strike three, a sound like the most powerful and delicious music in the world. But now, she stands before you, someone frankly you adore, and her hand comes up in a way that makes you think you should take it and walk with her into center field for a true picnic, but you know she wants the ball. It's all you had going for you and now she wants the ball.

Water Landings

Do not inflate your vest while still in the aircraft.

Those years
He had spent more time
Listening to the procedure
For water landings

Than he had
With the woman
He loved.

Advice on Finding Another Love Like Me

I want to tell you right now that you're going to have to look everywhere, and it is going to be tiring and frustrating, like if your knees
hurt and you still haven't looked down that one street, you're going to
have to go all the way down there and look around and under things
and I'll tell you right now, there's no love like me down there. Even
if you get an airplane and start looking over miles at a time looking
down on everything and everybody: no way. Look in the fancy places like where there's music playing while people shop and you'll find
nothing. Look in the library, but be quiet. Go into the stacks of books
and just look and look. Go skiing and look and the people passing in
the chairlifts two by two, no chance. Look on the internet like everyone else does and you'll find a jillion motes of nothing and searching
like that will wring your heart dry. I'm just saying. Ask your friends
and look at their friends. Oh they are totally going to show you their
friends, and what you'll see is their friends. Nice people, but what.
Is there a love like me among them? Several of those guys dress nice
and have modern hair, but seriously. Search for a phone booth and
look in the phone booth. If you can't find a phone booth, look in a tire
store waiting room where the coffee machine and magazines sit in
the little corner. Look in the train station out of nostalgia and look in
the train. Look in Sears and the pet store and why don't they sweep
the pet store? Look at the carnival and the people in line. Look in the
subway and in the army and the great open fields of unripened can-
taloupes. Use those big binoculars like in *Mission Impossible* or that
other film. Use a telescope. You are definitely going to need glasses
and then another pair of super glasses very soon. Your poor eyes
from looking! Oh go ahead and look in the post office and in the great
copper mine and alongside of the two lane highway. Keep searching.
Look in your dreams and on *America's Most Wanted*. Look in the hot

springs through the steam. Drink lots of water on your search and be careful driving, and from time to time remember the boy who loves you, who stands exactly where you haven't looked with a butter knife in his hand above the open jar waiting to see if you want marmalade and cheese on your toast. It's going to pop up in a minute, and he knows you like it warm.

After Surgery

The man was light-headed. His blood had run down to his feet, and he was waiting for it to return. That was what it seemed like. Or his knees. Someplace. When it returned the man planned to have an idea. It seemed like there was room for one. He certainly wanted an idea. He had woken, and there was work to do, not work, but like it. He'd had his heart out in the open air a few days ago. There were three or four people who had seen it, but he hadn't seen it. He'd been worried that it would still be him when he awoke. He awoke and he could drink apple juice, and he became for a short time a champion at drinking it. Ice-cold apple juice, like liquid gold, if liquid gold tasted like icy apples and dispersed in your body usefully. Then he wondered if he was still himself. He made a few sentences between the delicious stabbing sips of apple juice, and they seemed like something he might have said. Then a few people he loved called him by name. A good sign. I'm still myself, the man thought. But how will I be sure? What's the one thing that will nail it down? He tried to sing and he couldn't sing so that was good, because the man couldn't sing. He knew the words to only a few songs. He remembered the two poems he'd memorized before his heart was out and they were good poems. The good signs were adding up. Okay, so far so good. The nurse came and moved him to the side of the bed, and the man looked at his penis now and it looked strange, which was good, because his penis was strange before. The truth was that it was not strange, just some penis, but it did look familiar. He was pretty sure he'd seen it before. But where? He said that aloud, But where? And he laughed. It was like an old movie, a reunion of friends after some dire event. They'd been apart and concerned with other things far away and here they were on a street corner in London bumping into each other shocked and saying their names and can it be? Not

London but the hospital in Long Beach; it doesn't matter. They go to a pub for a drink and start to tell their stories. One of them is having trouble remembering and the other says, I see you like the apple juice. Now the man laughed in the hospital. Can I get you something the nurse said, and the man looked at her. It's me, he said. His heart had been in the open air but it had been returned to him. I'm so incredibly happy to be here.

II

Walk-bridge

—left foot, right foot—

Dwayne met me on the walk-bridge. I wasn't looking for him. I had been writing and I didn't exactly know where I was going. Then I learned that I had hoped not to run into him. I thought that meeting him on the narrow walk-bridge over the river was unfortunate. He seemed to be waiting for me, although he might have been simply standing on the bridge looking into the water thinking about something the way a man in a movie stands on a bridge, leaning against the iron rail. The man is contemplating something, a girl or something somebody said, or he's missing someone. These are the things I was thinking, and then I started doing some more accurate thinking and I knew that the man on the bridge was thinking about the guy who had walked his girlfriend home from the dance last Friday after he himself had passed out drunk from guzzling a bottle of sloe gin in the parking lot. The man was really thinking as he stared at the water. Nothing like a river to help a person think. It was certainly accelerating my thinking. I knew that I could not now turn around and run, for example, because I could see that would make the next meeting ten times whatever this one would be. Dwayne would find me down at the park, and that would be quite a meeting, especially with the two hours I would have to hide out down there thinking about it all, and this would be thinking without the help of the river. Then I did some crazy thinking there on the walk-bridge. For example: maybe he won't see me. I will just walk behind him and walk on. I adjusted my steps in accordance with such thinking to see if I could make them perfectly silent and I could not. Then I thought perhaps he wouldn't recognize me, but that was because I was having trouble recognizing myself in this situation. As I approached I saw Dwayne was making a fist. He was making a fist the way a man makes a bomb when it is a big bomb full of trouble and having many complicated color-coded wires which need to be attached to each other just so and in the right order and so the only way to proceed is step by step, and I saw Dwayne proceed step by step and fold each of his fingers into the bomb, I mean his hand, each finger tighter than the last and the dirty knuckles of his hand turning white with the new pressure as he completed making his fist and started making the second fist. When I made a fist it wasn't as effective as Dwayne's fist-making. In fact, I realized as I walked closer and closer to Dwayne on the walk-bridge over the river that I did not know how to make a fist. I'd never made a fist. I quickly scanned the history of my life for any fist moments, and there were none. I was not ready for this encounter. But maybe I was. If Dwayne saw me making a fist or he even saw what I called a fist with my fingers gathered loosely together like people come to see an accident, perhaps he would mistake me for being ready to fight which I was not. I had never been ready to fight. I don't know if this is a good trait or a bad trait, but it was my trait. I totally needed new traits.

When Dwayne's girlfriend Joylene, who I had known from drivers training, where there had been three of us on the four o'clock with Mr. Hunt, had come over to me and taken my hand at the dance last Friday night, that was when I should have known to make a fist or to do something with my hand that let her know it was a bad idea to drag me onto the gym floor to dance. As it was, I did some of my poorest thinking as I thought it was cool to hold her hand, to put my other arm around her waist as we moved slowly to the old song, "The Broken Moon" about the guy who is going to put the moon back together so he can make time go backwards to when he was with his girlfriend and they were happy. I mean, it is a nutty song, but there last Friday with me dancing with Joylene Wetherly under the flashing slivers of the prom ball for everyone to see, I thought it was the best song ever made, and I hoped the guy would get the moon fixed and that everything would be all right for him. Joylene smelled like the foyer of Gibson's, the department store where my mother gets my church shoes. On the walk-bridge, Dwayne turned to me as I walked up to him. I didn't know if I should stop or if I should just walk by like I had someplace to go, like I was getting home sort of fast on an errand, but he knew I was just going home from Leonard Rassels' where I had been playing Savage Henchmen for two hours. That's why he was on the bridge. He knew I would cut through the school to get to my place and he waited on the bridge. He turned to me, hauling his fists around on the ends of his arms like big cargo trucks being lifted around by cranes. He looked sort of funny that way, and if I knew him better I would have said, "Hey Dwayne, your fists are way too big for your body," but I didn't know him that well and now I was with him, face to face.

There are a lot of things I could have said right then, if I was going to speak first, such as "Hi, Dwayne," etc., as if I didn't know the purpose of his fists or I could have said, "There's no need to be mad at me for walking Joylene home. I was just there and nothing happened. I'm glad you're feeling better." I could never say the last. Or he could say something like, "What'd you do with Joylene?" Or: "What are you doing walking my girlfriend home?" And if either one of us would have spoken it would have led to a sketchy dialogue in which I would have tried like mad to talk about the things we had in common from when we played Pony League baseball together or flag football after school last fall. I would have been that guy trying to fix the moon so we could go back in time and avoid anything unpleasant.

Or perhaps we wouldn't talk, after all this thinking on my part, all this consideration of the history and options and my walk up the walk-bridge, and instead of any words we would have finally had his fists, first one of the big fists raised and then swinging through all of the air molecules between it and all the freckles on my nose. There would be a kind of relief in that fist moving in the atmosphere, a counterpoint, finally some action.

When they first built the walk-bridge across the little river so kids could walk directly to the junior high, we had gone down there, a bunch of us including my buddy Leonard Rassels and Dwayne and a lot of the kids from the neighborhood. Everyone likes a bridge. It was fabulous to finally walk right over the river! Late in the afternoon the newness was off it, and Dwayne pulled out some of his cigarettes, and I climbed up on the handrail, standing there. There were about four years in our neighborhood when we stood on everything. We climbed up and stood on things. Leonard had stood on the backstop in the park, and we'd been on the roof of every new and old garage for blocks. Dwayne pointed with his cigarette across the bridge and said to me: "Go for it." He meant I should tight walk across the handrail. He was a tough guy even then, and I liked that he was talking to me and I was good at walking on fence rails; I'd already been all the way around the park on that steel fence. So I started out up over the river and put one foot and then another on the black iron rail. I was looking down, and the brown river moving like it did silver and silver and silver made it real tough for a while. That's what it's like for me discovering a moment in writing, wanting to hurry and wanting to balance at the same time, feeling the full pressure of everything that could happen. I was so scared of Dwayne and his fists and the moment, but I was so excited to be there I can't even tell you.

Recommendation for Gordon Lee Bunson

It is a pleasure to write in behalf of Gordon Lee Bunson, who I have known for these past three semesters in which he has been my student in English 5000. I also have become acquainted with Mr. Bunson outside the classroom and feel I know him fairly well.

As his transcript shows, Gordon Lee, who likes to be called (and will only answer to) Demon and Demon Lee, has had some problems in English 5000. But as you are well aware, a transcript only tells part of any story. Mr. Bunson received an incomplete in his first attempt in my class, but you should know that all forty-seven students in that ill-fated section received incompletes. We were unable to finish the course because of a fire in our classroom, which consumed the entire basic English Wing of old Bracken Hall. In the event I suffered smoke inhalation to the degree that I lost my voice for over a month and could not carry on. But no one perished in the blaze, no doubt partly because of Mr. Gordon Lee Bunson's enthusiastic screaming and crying out, "This is some fire!" and "It's burning! It's burning!" In the confusion and excitement of the aftermath, Gordon Lee did confess to starting the fire, stating that he wanted everyone to know what "they could do with their nine hundred grammar rules" and all the parts of speech. It is essential to note that these remarks could not be used against him in a court of law, and they shouldn't now, except as they betray a kind of native intensity which is one of Mr. Bunson's strongest characteristics.

Mr. Bunson has transferred a great deal of his ardor toward me in the last few months, and he has completed several hundred handwritten notes to me. Most of these show a compelling and effective use of sentence fragments and phonetic spelling which have a unique energy. This prolific outburst can be seen as encouraging.

He is currently living in his car parked just a few feet from my house, and I've been able to observe Mr. Bunson's working habits. He's really quite remarkable—the kind of writer I would recommend to anyone. Using only the steering wheel as a desk and writing by the light of his cigarette, Mr. Lee has produced almost 30,000 words of a free-form novel, which features a person with my name as a hyperbolic antagonist. What an achievement! As a kind of performance piece, he's been leaving pages of this work taped to my front door every three or four hours.

This is a remarkable young man. Peering out the curtains I can see him even now adding to his opus, working night and day, eating and sleeping who knows when. This is an unusually well-motivated scholar. The energy and dedication here are without parallel and his liberal use of capital letters and scotch tape is also unique in my experience.

Listen, who cares about English 5000? Subject-verb agreement in our world has long been overrated. There is a man in a car outside my house, and I am recommending him to you with every bone in my body. Take him, please take him.

If I can offer any further information, please don't hesitate to call. Call me at home.

Recommendation for Cleo Descartes

It is a pleasure to write in behalf of my student Cleo Descartes, whom I have known here at Herdah College for the past year and a half. Ms. Descartes has been in my English 9000 class three semesters, and I feel I am capable of commenting on her academic abilities. English 9000, as the bulletin notes, is a thorough history of grammar, a close look at the three hundred and ninety grammar rules, which govern our eight and sometimes nine parts of speech. Passing the course is dependent on passing the three exams, all of which are multiple choice. I have some confidence that Cleo Descartes is going to pass English 9000 this term.

Her troubles with the comma, the semi-colon, and verb tense aside, Ms. Descartes has been a fairly good student. She is aware of some of her weaknesses and tries to take the appropriate action. For example, when Cleo comes to class this term she sits against the wall. This is the kind of tactic that more students should employ. She sits against the wall so that when I start speaking about the possessive pronouns and she falls asleep, she will not fall out of her chair onto her face as she did so often her first semester, with her skirt riding high up her backside revealing more of her thighs than any of the other young grammarians should really have had to witness.

When she sleeps in class, she sleeps quietly for the most part. From time to time there is a sonorous rhythmic snoring, very light, and actually not unpleasant. It sounds like a caravan of animals struggling over mountains in the distance. I want to quickly add that this is punctuated only from time to time by tortured staccato screaming: "I don't know what you're talking about!" and "No! No! I can't afford it!" These outcries are only periodic, as I noted, and because they are grammatically sound complete sentences for the most part, I give her partial credit for the class participation portion of our class. We in

English 9000 find these sudden and shrill moments stimulating, and many times I've used them to transition to my next topic.

Cleo Descartes is a personable, extremely polite young lady who would fit well in any graduate school environment. She stays after the bell rings and after all the other students have departed and frankly after I have left and turned the lights out. Without question, this focused young person has spent more time in our classroom this semester than any of her peers.

I urge you to give her every consideration.

Most sincerely,

Recommendation for Sterling Ogerladder

It is a pleasure to write in behalf of my student Sterling Ogerladder, who has been an absolute pleasure to know here at Herdah College. Mr. Ogerladder has been in six of my classes, including English 2000 (Penmanship, Grooming, and Etiquette), English 3000 (Co-authored novels of the 1970s), English 7000 (Introduction to the Literature of Atlantis), English 8600 and 8600 B (the year-long literary survey of Herdah County), English 9000 (Advanced Niceties of Grammar), and English 10000 (The Etymology of Contemporary Gambling Terms).

Sterling Ogerladder has been that student of whom every teacher dreams. He sits up straight and faces forward. He has his notebook open and he has his pencil in his hand. He has a faint smile on his face to indicate that he understands the little jokes we professors try from time to time. He is in his place when class commences and he stays until his professor leaves the room. He is, in other words, that rare thing: the ideal student.

I was as surprised as anyone this last term when it was discovered that Sterling Ogerladder had no pulse, and evidently has been in this state for almost two years now. I guess he passed away sometime in his sophomore year. It makes sense. The classes he took with me were all in lecture hall 248, and he always wore the same sweater. I for one am not going to hold this medical condition against him. He continues to be one of the most focused students I've ever encountered. I'm recommending him to you with genuine enthusiasm. He looks good sitting there and he won't smirk like so many of the undergraduates these days. I'm told that if you admit Mr. Ogerladder, you'll also get his desk and personal effects.

Please call me if I can be of further assistance.

At times students have wondered at the meaning of some of the codi-
fied marginalia on their stories written in English 5000, Introduction
to Fiction Story Writing. This style guide should answer the most fre-
quently asked questions.

CIRCLED WORD: What is this word? Replace with any known word.

EXCLAMATION POINT: Is this a believable act? Do you mean to have the man stop crying after just one night and get on with his life? The young woman left only a week ago. Is this the nature of grief?

QUESTION MARK: You're being too symbolic here. Can there be a rainbow over the tree by the riverbank? Can those clouds have silver linings? Are clouds lined? Are the birds in this scene singing? Are you sure? Are you such an ornithologist that you can distinguish bird song from avian cries of hunger, fear, or anguish?

CW: Name the woman Cheryl as suggested in the Cheryl Whitcomb Lecture (Week 3).

STAR: Why do you have the stars shining in this scene? Do you understand that they are distant raging infernos that don't give two hoots about human interactions? They don't cross and uncross like little bright symbols of fate. The constellations themselves are mankind's desperate attempt to cast a feeble metaphoric net over the universe.

LITTLE SMILEY FACE: Let's not forget the little guy, the guy that stays behind, who writes letters day after day with stubborn faith and persistent love and the same old red pen he uses to mark his students' papers.

BIG SMILEY FACE: Put the Mayor in the background of this scene.

LEFT-HANDED CHECK: A small tic I've developed while reading sex scenes.

LEFT-HANDED CHECK WITH A BOX AROUND IT: Note to myself to reread this section.

SMALL CASE CW: The young woman in the scene should be a little more like Cheryl Whitcomb; see Cheryl Whitcomb lecture notes, weeks 2, 3, 4, and 5.

TREBLE CLEF: Isn't your use of music a bit melodramatic? Are you a writer dependent on soundtrack?

BIG CIRCLED T: Let's avoid the present tense.

SMALL X: Ignore this mark: something in the scene has reminded me to add an item to my grocery list: mustard, fresh lettuce, shaving cream, ginger.

CAPITAL X: My willingness to read further has expired.

CAPITAL CW: Please: make this female character more like Cheryl Whitcomb; second warning.

K: Awkward

UT: Untoward

BACKWARD K: Backward

CW: Make the girl here a little more like Cheryl Whitcomb; see your notes on the Cheryl Whitcomb Lecture from weeks 2, 3, 4, and 5.

LITTLE SQUIGGLE: This is the British spelling, please adjust.

DOUBLE SQUIGGLE UNDER A CW: Great opportunity to make this woman like Cheryl Whitcomb.

TRIPLE SQUIGGLE ON EACH SIDE OF A CW: Cheryl Whitcomb would hardly act this way; please rewrite.

WCW: You are close to being right here, but the female character wouldn't carry a handbag without a shoulder strap. . . . Would Cheryl Whitcomb?

HAIR!: You've got a strand of hair in the woman's face which she keeps brushing behind her ear; I don't think so, refer to the hairstyle section of the Cheryl Whitcomb lectures.

LITTLE CLOCK WITH A SLASH ACROSS ITS FACE: You may not say "It seemed like forever," or "It seemed like eternity," in this scene. If your character is waiting for a call or a letter or a smile or a kind word from Cheryl Whitcomb, you can say that it seemed like forever or it seemed like an eternity. You may not invoke forever, the twelfth of never, eternity, infinity, or never-ending for any other activity. If the character in your scene is in her tenth hour of labor indicate that by saying it seemed like ten hours.

STATUS LIFE OR $: You've got to do some work on your female characters. There is no way on this great green earth that Cheryl Whitman would ever be a data entry operator, and that's not her car. Perhaps you remember the Cheryl Whitcomb apartment inventory lecture. Do you remember any worn penny oxfords? A Green Bay Jersey? Curlers? Neither do I.

WATERMARK, TEARSTAIN, TORN PAPER: Let's go ahead and get rid of this character, the boyfriend or whatever you're calling him. Get him and his ridiculous letter jacket out of her building. See the Cheryl Whitcomb Lecture, Fidelity Appendix, sections 4 through 19. There is no boyfriend.

RED X, LARGE RED X, OR OPEN PUNCTURE THROUGH PAPER: No fiancé. Lose him. Let's take this young broker and his diamond ring in its velvet box and write a scene where he has an unfortunate jaywalking incident with a garbage truck. Name him Rudyard and run him over. The Cheryl Whitcomb character can scream, but just once before she gets back to her office.

PENTAGRAM RADIATING SHINING GOO-GAHS: The First Amendment was not intended to protect people writing what you are writing when you have a character such as you do, who bears so many of the Cheryl Whitcomb characteristics, and you have her go into a bar like the Silly Philly. If you don't change the scene where she goes up and sits at the bar and orders a Furtrader with a beer back, you will fail this class and I'll have you arrested before you can leave the building.

AMPERSAND: Please coordinate your conjunctions properly here.

SMALL Y: Yes! Yes! Yes! This is good good work. Your plot points are well measured. Cheryl Whitcomb's office is done just right. When the Cheryl Whitcomb character finishes at her desk, it's late and she swivels once in her chair and looks out the glassy expanse of her window onto the shimmering city beneath her. That's right: it's an old Slim Whitman CD playing softly. She's just finished the big case that will save so many innocent people and put the evil developer where he belongs along with his drug smuggling flunkies. Yes, there is an air of satisfaction, but no smugness. Yes, she's happy to be doing good, but there in her eye is the right touch of loneliness too. Yes, just right. Before she stands up and grabs her valise, she takes one small moment, her only indulgence and she thinks of him, her one true love, lost so long ago. She pictures him in his old Hush Puppies, not unlike my own, standing in class in a small college far away. His jacket is smudged with chalk and he's gesturing with enthusiasm to his captivated students. Such a noble calling, teaching; he must be an angel. Cheryl Whitcomb sighs deeply. The bright city means nothing to her. Yes, you've got it right. She stands in the dark office and puts her forehead against the cool glass and closes her eyes. The stars above flicker knowingly. Her true love writes on the blackboard somewhere. He passes back papers to his eager and admiring students. Birds sing. Some gather on his shoulders. She wonders if he ever—for a moment—thinks of her.

ADV: Replace with an adverb.

AGR: Pronoun agreement problem

PLUS SIGN: Not bad, pretty good, keep typing.

My MOOC

We let go of calling roll after the first time, as it took us most of three weeks. I had seventy thousand, four hundred and sixty-one students, and so we went right to the honor system. We did a lot of things in this MOOC with the honor system. For instance when I asked if those in the back could hear me, I took the one small fire I could see there on the horizon to signify that they could. I asked them to put the fire out, and that was accomplished pretty directly, and the smoke sort of let me know where the back row was. Maybe a quarter mile, I'm not sure. I am sure that my handouts didn't make it that far. I could see my students' faces flickering in the light of their screens which made it look to me like we were really learning something. Several people were tardy, and it took weeks for them to arrive. Of course, I gave a lecture, one of my best, on the responsibility of the individual in society and the power of the individual to change things, etc. and make a difference in so many ways and I listed the ways, the ones I could remember. From time to time I paused when there were disturbances in the assembled students. I couldn't tell if they were nodding in agreement or fighting in their various factions. I saw hands raised, or sticks, something. It was a lively session. Evaluating their papers posed a special challenge. I'm an experienced teacher and had read and marked papers all of my life, but never more than thirty-seven at a time. When the trucks arrived at my house with the first term papers, we had what I'll call an educational moment. I finally had the drivers stack all of this advanced writing on the walkway along the hedge by my front door and in the street. Immediately upon the trucks' departure, the wind urged great stacks of the manuscripts against my front door and I could see them drifting there like snow, though I could not open the door for fear of being crushed. I used my binoculars from the window to read several of the papers and from what I could tell, we seemed to be on the right track, though I may have to wait for a more powerful weather system to come through so I can gain exit from my house. When the wind does carry some of these well-typed manuscripts down the street, I think of it as meeting one of my hoped for outcomes: spreading the word, the true dissemination of knowledge.

My Soldiers

Most of the time when I write something, a scene or a description, it all comes out perfect the first time, just exactly right, like a phalanx of golden soldiers marching down the King's Highway, well, not a phalanx but an organized group of soldiers in clean and shiny uniforms, and really not soldiers but say some committee of beautiful citizens, yes that's more like it and they are gleaming as they proceed down the King's Highway, though I see now it is more like the Garden Path, a dirty byway that wends its tender way through the great fields of orchids growing there, and so: perfect. There they are the committee of beautiful citizens strolling through the fragrant country, and they begin to talk, that is say things, well, wrangle really and argue. It is a committee, a word now I see is all wrong. It's more like a club of like-minded individuals, men and women and maybe some children who are also like-minded, and they are stumbling along in the dirt, arguing about the direction the club has been going for a few years, ever since they elected the one guy chairman: Ron. And now they stop and gather around him angrily, and their boots are muddy, and you can see from their boots that this is not a club but a gang and to call them like-minded is possibly a mistake. In fact, the only thing they have in common is that they are armed, and these are crude weapons, fence posts and rocks and fistfuls of orchid petals, stamens, like that. Their remarks are casual and full of agreement errors and their remarks are loud and not made in accordance with *Robert's Rules of Order*. Robert is not among them. In fact, now I see I recognize no one among them, even the one woman with the great vampire bat tattooed on her shoulder. Darkness is coming. There would have been twilight or evening in another paragraph, but now it is just dark, and the sour smell of rotting flowers drifts over this mob. They are encouraged and animated by the darkness, and now I can't see what they are doing, but can only guess at these actions and try to listen for the cries of distress.

Most of the time when I write something, it comes out perfect, but there are actually some times when I go back and change a word or two.

My Maladies

Honestly, I was hoping to have a conversation, but my maladies have come between me and that possibility. My maladies, not to make a long song and epic dance out of it, but my maladies have afflicted me aplenty. It might help if I describe them, the way I did to the medical professionals: first, I had some backup which slowed down the server. I'd already had a virus or two, and I thought this was just my system operating, but then I started to blog, and that was terrifically unpleasant. Plus it is rude and embarrassing. I'd be somewhere and suddenly: blog. No, really: people don't like that. It's like an unwanted opinion: blog. I knew then what I know now: it wasn't natural. Pretty soon it wasn't occasional, but I was fully blogging. Some of my blogs were linked. People, my friends, knew I was blogging and I couldn't tell them differently. After I had blogged there were people who examined my blog and sometimes there was matter in my blog which just upset everyone. No one wanted to have me blogging; as my best friend said, "If you've seen one blog, you've seen them all."

All this time I was steadily downloading, and then with my blog in full-blown blog mode, I began to podcast. I had a feeling something was happening, and then it did. Podcasting was horrible. Pods! There I'd be, looking normal, but suddenly I'd cast a pod. I wasn't used to this at all. I was casting pods everywhere, literally. The professionals were just confused by this and for a while they supported me. Cast that pod, they'd say. Don't let them back up on you. Well, I'd been backing up the server. Now they said: podcast if you can. I didn't want everyone to see my pods. But I could not stop casting them. Then my maladies achieved their current dimension which has caused me so much alarm. I started casting blogs. It was bad enough to blog, but then to cast them. And then I began to blast clogs which made no one laugh out loud. My heavens.

Now, I'm blogging pods and that's disgusting. A blog-covered pod is more than I can stand. It's hideous. I'm podding blogs and blogging casts. My maladies are such that now I'm all atwitter and I cannot even podcast in a straight line. Of course, I've omitted out of good taste the fact that all through my maladies I was also streaming in real time. And I also had several websites. Plus, all along I had been getting hits. These are the final stages so far, the professionals say.

There are other maladies to come, I'm told. It's worldwide, of course, a pandemic. Everybody has it. We can't even talk to each other anymore without a website casting a pod. I miss everyone. I just want to sit down and talk, to have a conversation, and I'm waiting for these maladies, blog, pod, tweet, to pass.

Teaching Evaluation

This professor was consistent, I'll say that. He moved
the overhead projector every day at the beginning of class.
The classroom was used for overhead projection in the hour
before our class, and the overhead projector was always left
in the middle of the room. But this professor moved it
out of the way. Do you see what I'm saying?
He never used the overhead projector because in Grammar 9000,
there is little need for projection overhead.
That's what he told us. It wouldn't have been too bad
to have had some of the parts of speech projected overhead,
or maybe some dependent clauses, but who knows?
It would have been nice to turn off the lights just once
and have anything projected overhead.
The other class had used the overhead projector.
But our professor knew better. Of course,
when you are sitting in Grammar 9000
and being pounded with the ten-ton history of verb tenses,
including the subjunctive which he told us was not
present reality or future certainty, but a possibility
mediated by someone's desire;
it does sound delicious to sit in a darkened classroom listening
to the overhead projector hum softly while you look at anything
at all on the one bright wall: a diagram of angel's wings
or a molecular diagram of rust
or the elevations in Yosemite, projected overhead.
A lot of Grammar 9000 was over my head, frankly,
even though English is my first language. I swear to god it is.
He unplugged it and then my professor would wrap the cord
before he moved the overhead projector. He planned ahead like that.

Then he would push it on its cart with such care
that it just gave us all confidence. Hey: he was not going to crash
or damage that overhead projector, ever,
and he must have moved it fifty times. He parked it in the corner
every day, and when it was safe and out of the way,
this guy, our professor, turned to us.

III

Dangerous Relics

It wasn't that the relics themselves were dangerous, although they sometimes had splinters or if you dropped a relic it could hurt your foot, especially in the sandals we sometimes had to wear, but there was always danger around the relics, and the biggest danger was the dragons. The dragons were just what you'd expect: big reptiles that could bite and harass and irritate and harm you. They also had claws some of them and wings and a barbed tail and about half of the dragons could breath fire out upon you if you neared the relics. The dragons could not be tamed, and their powers could not be mitigated. When they opened their blood-shot eyes and spied you, they would stand up and start right in. The thing about the dragons was that they were always really people who had turned themselves into dragons or who had been turned into dragons. A few of these people were reluctant to be dragons, and it was hard to tell about the others. It was also terribly confusing to figure out how they'd become dragons. Sometimes it was a totem or a curse or an amulet or a charm. It was never DNA; we looked into this. Sometimes it was an ankh, which was also confusing. It was hard to know where to put that H. The relics themselves also had power. Of course. That is why everyone was in search of relics. There wasn't an unending supply, but there were plenty. If you could get the right relic, it might be the key to rewriting the myth. That was the goal: to rewrite the myth. What if you secured the relic that indicated north was south? That would change things. Certain people wanted that to be true and searched for the relic. Other people, some who were dragons already, wanted things to stay the same and they defended the relic by flying around it shooting fire on interlopers. I wasn't sure if we wanted to rewrite the myth, but I did enjoy searching for relics. I wanted to do something. This way, I got to go into castles and caves and grottoes, special places you don't see every day. Many people found relics and rewrote the myths based on what they found and then they discovered they had fake relics. Fake relics were trouble and they looked so good! Some old rusty bolt or big iron key which sort of glows in the lamplight could be fake. A piece of dirty linen could be fake. Linen was always fake. Some rag and everybody's ready to rewrite the myth. Regardless, the myth got rewritten and then that got rewritten and it was all based on relics and fake relics. You could pretty much choose which myth you wanted and then back it up with a relic. I felt bad about those relic seekers who got burned up by dragons who were defending fake relics. The best thing you could do with a fake relic was hide it behind two or three smoking dragons. The presence of dragons made any old relics seem real; dragons were better than antique varnish for making a relic seem real. I should say that I found some things, bits of wood and a leather brace with a red jewel in it, and I kept those things. I considered using them to rewrite the myth, but I didn't want to. I didn't want to rewrite anything. I wanted to go to some grottoes I'd heard of over the hills and work in the mysteries there.

When the Monster Is Actively Moving toward You—How to Start the Car

Shut your door and turn the key. The car will growl as the starter rotates, but the engine will not start. It will sound like: nuuhhnn, nuuhhn, nuhhhh. Pound the top of the steering wheel with both hands and say or call out, "Come on! Come on!" Now, again turn the key in the ignition. It will not start. Continue to make the same noise as before. Pound the steering wheel a few more times, hard, with your left hand while you continue turning the key with your right hand. Call out loudly now, "Come on!" and "Not now!" If you feel like it, you can embellish this with, "You stupid car!" and or "You piece of junk!" Don't analyze it all too much or yell out, "Why didn't I get the engine serviced or check the battery or buy better gasoline!" It is not a great time for this kind of inquiry. Besides, it might be the solenoid or the starter motor whatever that is. Cars are a mystery, face it. It's easier to understand where the monster originated than how a car even works. It's easier by far to understand why the monster wants to get you. He's been coming for you for a long time. He's been patient, actually. You sort of deserve the monster; that's the really terrifying part. You totally deserve the monster. Now you should continue to groan and yell and pound the top of the steering wheel as much as you can. When you feel the monster arrive, either by feeling a force you never imagined take hold of the back bumper or by making close visual contact through your open window, roll that window up to the best of your ability. The monster is going to try to prevent you from rolling up the window. Be persistent and act like it's not your monster, like there might be some mistake and say the words, "No no no no no no." The monster is going to be on the other side of the glass watching you pretty closely. Try the key, turn the key. Pound the steering wheel. Try the key. Nuuhhh. Nunnnhh.

Nunh. Then: when the engine roars to life like a lion provoked at last, you'll be crying. If you want you can say now, "Why me? Why me?" a few times. But we know the answer to that. Open your door and slide over so the monster can drive. It's all right. He knows where you were going. He's known all along.

How to Be a Man

When you move left for a hard-hit ground ball and misplay it and it goes between your legs and on into left field allowing the runner on third to score the winning run, don't look in your mitt as if the ground ball which would have saved the day is in there because it is not. Stand up straight and remove your glove and carry it by the thumb in your off hand. Walk with your chin at altitude toward the dugout. Keep your eyes open. Do not grimace. Look for the coach's face and when you find it, look him in the eye and nod. You know what happened.

The Captain's Daughter

We were with the captain in headquarters when the radio call came in. The creature was on B deck. The captain checked his pistol and said to me, Let's go. We were both tired of waiting.

His daughter said, I'm going with you.

You stay here, Kristen.

I'm going. I want to be part of this.

No. It's too dangerous.

I'm going.

Stay here.

I'm going with you. I can help.

Stay here; it's too dangerous.

I want to go.

No. Stay here. We'll handle this.

I can handle it.

No, you stay.

I can shoot a gun.

You can't go.

I'm going with you.

Sit down and stay here. We'll go.

I'm going with you.

Stay here.

I can help.

You need to stay here.

I'm going to be part of this.

You are not! Stay put. We'll be right back.

I've come this far. I'm not waiting in the background.

You must wait.

I'm going. You can't stop me.

Yes I can. You're not going.

I'm going with you.

Stay!

You can't make me stay.

It's too dangerous!

I'm an expert with a javelin.

Wait here.

You're going to need me.

Sit!

You can't talk to me that way.

We've got to go.

And take me with you.

You stay here.

You can't make me stay.

Stop.

You're not in charge of me.

It's fraught with jeopardy.

I'm coming.

We're all going to perish. You remain here.

I'm fast and alert and I will be an asset.

Stay here and we'll come back for you.

I won't be here because I'll be with you.

No. You must remain.

I'll take notes and send messages.

Stay here.

My knot-tying abilities will be necessary.

You are not coming along. We must hurry.

I can hurry with you.

You wait for us.

I'm ambidextrous.

We'll be right back.

Keep an eye out and we'll do this fast.

I'm coming with you. Don't you see?

We'll be right back.

I know because I'll be with you.

We've got to go.

I'm coming. I speak French.

You stay here.

No! You stay here, I'll go.

We don't have time for such talk.

Then let's go.

Yes, we are going, but without you.

With me.

We'll be back in ten minutes or twenty.

I'm going with you; let me go.

You must remain behind as my daughter.

That's why I must go. I'll stand behind you.

The daughter doesn't go.

That's an old idea. This is the new world. I'm going.

Stay here. Wait for us. Wait here.

You're not leaving me here. Not now.

This thing has torn men apart!

I don't care! I'm coming.

It's bad news. You wait here.

I know hypnosis. You'll need me.

Where'd you learn hypnosis?

It was a correspondence course and part of it was online.

Was it that Dr. Respondo e-mail we all got?

What if it was?

I told you to stay away from Dr. Respondo. Did you charge it to your credit card?

None of your business. And Dr. Respondo's class was beautiful.

Did you meet him in person after corresponding on the internet?

Yes, yes I did. So what? He treats me like an adult.

You're my daughter. I don't want you consorting with Dr. Respondo.

Well too bad. We're engaged.

Show me the ring.

He doesn't believe in rings. We have a shared tattoo.

Did you just hypnotize me?

Yes.

That's low. That is poor form.

I don't care what you say. Dr. Respondo told me to use my powers.

Fair enough stay here. We'll be right back.

Don't be long. I'll wait right here.

Sky King

The bad guy gets the drop on Sky King. Hands up and all the rest. The big gun in the small cabin in the mountains. They call it getting the drop on somebody when you have them covered with a gun. Sky King has his hat on. He always has his hat on. There is no reason the bad guy does not shoot. If it were any other person, that person would shoot, but not the bad guy with the drop on Sky King. Penny, Sky King's daughter, is flying *Songbird*, their plane, toward the mountain landing strip right now unaware of the danger. Her job is to be unaware of the danger. Of course the bad guy doesn't want to be caught. He's spent his entire life doing things that he doesn't want to be caught for. It would have been better had he just got a job, even a good janitorial job or road work, and showed up every day for a few years until he felt invested and had friends he ate lunch with and bowled and complained in the joking manner of other men. But no, he's a bad guy and he's trying to take some vile shortcut to riches, usually riches. This is the fifties and the bad guys are unshaven but not creepy. This is Sky King. The bad guys want the treasure, even though they have no claim to it. In fact, right now with Sky King's hands in the air, the treasure sits by the bunk bed in a box which could only hold treasure. It's not a box at all, but a crafted wooden chest with brass ribs and fittings and a big lock in the hasp. It's called a strongbox. Still the bad guy does not shoot. Evidently, he wants to gloat. It's a human trait we all share, but seeing it in others is unpleasant. The bad guy waves his gun in little circles. This is brandishing. He's brandishing his weapon, a huge, classic six shooter with a revolving cylinder and a pearl handle, a gun a boy would want. He's brandishing and gloating when Sky King says his line. His line is: *Don't look behind you, Smithy*. This is a great moment. Sky King has introduced a variable no one counted on. It implies that one of Sky King's allies, perhaps Penny or Scooter, is behind Smithy standing there with a silver pistol and the drop on Smithy. Smithy's nervousness doubles. Or triples, some multiplier. Will Smithy fall for the ruse? Is it a ruse? We don't even have the word ruse; it's 1955. Ike is in the White House and the French have just left Vietnam. I'm seven and ride my bike down to the river with Fenn even though I'm forbidden, and we throw rocks at debris floating by and pretend to smoke the dry reeds and watch the older kids from the other neighborhood swim. At home my mother asks me where I've been and I say, At the park, and she turns to her errands. These are my first lies.

In Sky King, Smithy, the bad guy, does one of the following. He says, *You're not going to get me with that old trick Sky King.* If he says this there are two scenarios. In one there is definitely one of Sky King's allies standing behind him, gun ready, sometimes Penny. Penny will say, *Oh yeah, Smithy, drop your gun,* and he will drop his gun. They were always dropping their guns. Or, two, when he says *You're not going to get me with that old trick, Sky King,* it actually is the old trick and there is no one behind Smithy and when he looks to be sure, urged by his new nervousness, Sky King will pounce upon him righteously and punch him into submission, western-style. Smithy didn't shoot Sky King because it would have not allowed him to explain his crime and reveal where he's tied up the innocent hostages and hidden the horses. He tied the twins in the mine to the box of dynamite and he laughs at his cleverness. He's sort of got a point: the twins were obnoxious with their questions all day long to Sky King like, Can I fly *Songbird?* and How high are we now, Sky? And he hid the horses by the creek ready for his getaway with the strongbox. He brandishes his big gun and talks away, every twist in his wicked story. Smithy never uses the brandishing interview to reflect on his life as a bad guy, citing his first bad deed and how it troubled him but he kept on and how he regrets many of his crimes and rues the loneliness his life as a bad guy has delivered unto him. He'd like a companion, a nice woman to care for him, heat the water so he could finally shave, but what kind of woman wants a bad guy? If he talked like that, he'd just drop the gun and sit on the strongbox and weep, and Sky King would have to pull off his own bandana and give it to Smithy for his horrid runny nose. We always hope when Sky King says, *Don't look behind you, Smithy*, that the trick will work, or even if it is not a trick, we hope it will work. The twins are tied up in the mine, and the fuse is burning.

Sky King was a pilot and he flew the Arizona skies. The way he escaped from trouble made me wonder if there would always be something behind me, real or imagined, that would change things when the time came.

How Things Have Actually Changed Since We Did Secede from the United States

The Rubynars keep dropping in. Just like always, they come to this side of town for the laundromat or one of Travers's soccer games and they drop in, two bleeps on the horn and where's the coffee? It's been our custom until now, but customs are changing if you haven't noticed. Now we have a Customs Office. Or will have.

This time I hear their horn and I hurry out to the curb where they've parked, and I explain to Norman Rubynar that they would need a visa if they were going to cross onto the property; we've seceded, and I can't tell you how important our borders are to us. I give the entire carful of Rubynars my "borders speech," Norman and Travers and Beesley and Shirley, who has been my best friend since twenty-two years ago and the first day at Babnab Junior High. The speech traces in oratory how I once lived in a big fat land that grew complacent and had no respect for its own borders, and in that sad principality we were overrun by who knows what when, and so our family seceded, and now that our family has seceded the Rubynars and everybody else, especially Carl and Janice Poline are going to need visas to cross onto our country, our property, and here I wave our deed at them and tell them our visa office won't be open for weeks. At least. We've spent too much time developing our postal system, and I've taken a good boatload of guff for our stamps, which Janice Poline was snotty enough to point out look like Pokémon stickers, but they are not. They are modified Pokémon stickers and let's just say you're going to need one to get any mail in or out of Gundersonia, land of the really free. They are not that expensive and they come with a list of our zip codes, one for each of the girls. Doug and I decided to share one.

Norman and Shirley Rubynar sit in the truck and drink their coffee and Norman lets Biggee into the truck with them and strokes his ears and asks me doesn't the dog need a visa? Of course he doesn't need a visa, I tell these bohemians: he's the National Dog. Shirley sits in the front seat trying not to spill her coffee. It sort of feels like a foreign land, she says. Oh it is, I tell her. We got no gay marriage and we got the English only. Travers is squirming in the back seat and I can see they better be going. Can't he use the bathroom? Shirley says. We won't make it home. I can't allow it, I tell them. It is a slippery slope. We got our sovereignty to think of. One undocumented visit to the toilet and next the borders are awash in who knows what. Travers has got no driver's license or green card and he'll need a bank account and employment to even apply. What about a letter from the Pope? Norman says. It's the kind of comment which strains international relations to the limit.

In Jeddah

The American rode in the van up the coast. The sky was bright, and the highway went north in Jeddah, past many monuments, the giant camels, the balanced globe, the car on the flying carpet. Jeddah was full of sculpture, and the American looked at all of it. His father had been a sculptor in Arizona, welding huge eagles out of steel with a torch. The American missed his father very much; they had been close friends. And his father would have loved to hear about the American's time in Saudi Arabia.

Now the van arrived at the beach club, and the gate opened. The American paid 70 reals to enter, and for this he received permission to swim and a ticket to an ice cream cone. The American loved ice cream. He had been lonely a great deal in the last three years and he had used ice cream to overcome some of his loneliness. It was wonderful company even though it never lasted long.

The American was with friends today and so he wasn't lonely. He hadn't been lonely in all of Saudi Arabia. In Riyahd, there had been no time to be lonely. They were always meeting Saudis and speaking to them about writing. The American was a writer and had been writing all of his life, and one of his favorite things was to talk to other writers about what they were creating. Writing is creating. That was what the American knew they all had in common, a desire to create and a desire to be understood. The American wanted to be understood by others, of course, and he had had some trouble understanding himself at times in his life.

He walked with his friends toward the sea. They placed their watches and cameras and towels and shirts on the teak-wood lounge chairs and they stepped into the brimming sea. The water made the man smile. He loved the ocean. He was big in his love for the ocean. He loved all the oceans, and there are supposedly seven oceans, but the American secretly thought there might be more. He had never ever been in the Red Sea and now he was in the Red Sea. A bright blue-and-green fish with yellow fins brushed his leg, and the American looked into the water and said to the fish, Hello to you too.

His friends swam out into the Red Sea, and the American swam out in the warm water. The wind was blowing. It wanted to blow them all back to the city, but they swam against the wind. I am in the Red Sea, the man said to himself. He was smiling and happy to be in this rare place. Because he was a writer, he thought it might make a nice story for someone he loved.

After swimming and observing the many bright fish in the reef, the American crawled back toward the stone steps and felt himself cut his foot on the coral. He did it twice and then again. When he walked out of the sea, his foot was bleeding. He was glad to see the red blood from the little scratches. It is good to be reminded of your body, though it was embarrassing to have this little injury.

Traveling far from home is often prized and celebrated, and it is a valuable endeavor, but it always has an element of loneliness in it. The American sat with his friends drying off after swimming in the Red Sea. They were laughing and telling stories and they even took a photograph of their scratched feet. He was not alone in cutting his feet. And now the American, who was already happy to be in the wondrous country of Saudi Arabia, and happy to have these pictures and the story he would tell, knew something else. He knew he would now have a sweet walk back to the van, and on the way there with his friends there would be ice cream.

An Epic Epithalamion for Ashley and Ryan

Oh sing in me muse and through me tell the story
or the poem of the meaning of this event
or at least help me with some rhymes in my epic verse
so it doesn't get much worse or require a nurse,
okay that's enough with the rhyming—
epic Muse or not—
although I liked the nurse, another woman in white.

An epic poem of course has an epic catalogue of weapons
like the inventory list on Gears of Warfare, but this is
a marital and not a martial event, and we'll let that go—
although it would have been cool to list some fancy boats
or some gigantic swords like with the gleaming gold and such.

The participants hereabouts, that is Ashley and Ryan, to name names,
have walked up the aisle at long last after many valiant struggles
or so it says in the big book, but that could have been a misprint,
perhaps for snuggles, they've endured epic snuggles.
They've snuggled here and there, and their manifold snuggling
has led them at long last like any great journey, boats or no,
to the end of the aisle. And this is sure to be the launching pad
for a million snuggles to come or so we're all imagining.
Not launching pad, but something like that.

Ryan will give his hand in marriage,
and an arm and a leg, excuse my language,
Ashley will give Ryan the benefit of a doubt,
which as anyone knows is the benefit

we all require. It's better than dental insurance, as benefits go.
Even better than the optical option, the one I read.

They've exchanged vows. A vow for a vow.
It's the last time they can be exchanged.
You can exchange glances, right now, if you'd like;
go ahead and glance the bride, glance the groom,
but you can't give these vows back.
That's why you've snuggled all the way
to this blessed aisle,
to do something permanent,
something no inventory of weapons
or rhyming muse can mutate.
A vow for a vow: epic.

My Favorite Martian

I'm just not going to play that game,
favorites, like who's the favorite and all that,
and everybody wants to know who's favorite
when it's always a close call and as if having
a favorite would help anything as if there was
a prize or some glorious favorite honor and so I'm just
going to say all the Martians are my favorites,
everyone from Mars is my favorite, seriously
every Martian equal.
           I should add right here
that actually you're my favorite Martian. Seriously.
You are totally from Mars and for several reasons
that I am aware of you are my favorite.

IV

Horror Story at Lonely Lake

It was a red boat and it attacked people at Lonely Lake. People would be swimming in the alcoves of the lake, and the boat would attack. It ran over people anytime it wanted to. If there was a waterskier and he fell down into the water of Lonely Lake or there was a woman waterskier who fell, the red boat would run over them, and its propeller would chop them up until they were hard to look at, and their stories were hard to hear. If there was a fisherman just wading in the shallow parts of Lonely Lake, the boat would attack. It would go by as if just boating and then it would attack the fisherman. It attacked boats sometimes and ran into them and cut them in half, and when the people spilled into the water of Lonely Lake, the red boat would turn in determined circles until it had run over all of the people even if they were screaming for help. If they were calling, the boat still ran over them. It attacked at night or in the daytime. In the evening people listened. It was scary at night on Lonely Lake, but the days were just as dangerous. It attacked canoes and rowboats and it attacked the old scout troop in their inner tubes. The red boat was the worst thing about Lonely Lake. If someone mentioned Lonely Lake, then someone also said *red boat.*

Once a year the search party went out to try to find the red boat and destroy it so it would stop attacking people in Lonely Lake. It was always a methodical search and went around the whole lake, from the earthen dam at the north end all the way to the swampy sloughs at the south end. They looked into all the boat houses, private ones and the big club boathouse and they looked into the abandoned boathouses and under the old Sycamore Bridge, which is also abandoned. They searched under the great willow shelf on the west side and the sandy beaches on the east side. They always found a lot of lost gear and some dinghies which had floated off and canoes, but they never found the red boat which attacked people on Lonely Lake.

We tried to figure out why it was attacking. We had a town meeting in the lodge at Lonely Lake, and Mr. Blister stood at the blackboard and printed out the reasons.

Mrs. Abletable stood and said, "The boat attacks because it is evil." In the lighted lodge under the great stuffed moose, this made sense and everyone in the room nodded and agreed, and we made a sound together of agreement.

Mr. Blister wrote "EVIL."

Mr. Bakertaker raised his hand and said, "Maybe it is the Devil's Boat." That really hit a chord of agreement in the room, and we all spoke to each other and said *That is so true. I agree,* and like that, and Mr. Blister wrote "Devil's Boat" on the blackboard.

It was the blackboard from the Mercantile which occupies the front of the Lonely Lake Lodge and it usually had the produce specials on it in Mr. Blister's loopy printing. We all liked his printing. You could trust it.

Then Mrs. Candlewandle said, "I think that boat is out for revenge. It attacks everything because of something that happened a long time ago. That's the way these things work. Something terrible happened in the long lost history of Lonely Lake, and that red boat continues to seek its revenge." The logic of this comment made us gasp.

Mr. Blister wrote on the board: "Revenge."

Mr. Dordlenordle stood up and said, "I think the boat isn't the Devil's Boat, but some lesser demon here to terrify Lonely Lake. I think the devil himself is too busy for an old small place like this." The reasoning here was outstanding, and we all hummed approval.

Mr. Blister wrote down "Demon" on the board. The meeting was just getting started, and there was a sense of accomplishment already. You get a man in the clean well-lighted lodge writing on the blackboard in big letters, and it feels like you're finally getting somewhere. In an hour the blackboard was full of ideas, good ideas, including some scientific theories which included physics and chemistry.

We had refreshments of cool punch and oatmeal cookies and talked until almost ten o'clock. It was the whole town, everybody taking a turn, Mrs. Hindlebindle and Mr. Markennarken and Mr. Stoppermopper and Mrs. Vankerlanker, and I mean everybody with their stupid names and their passionate theories and all of us humming our agreement after every ardent remark until you could see it in every eye in the old room, hatred, and the deep dark hope that the red boat would find Mr. OckleFockle and Mrs. FerdyHerty, any of these people, and chop them into little bloody wicklenickles. Our esteem for the red boat was gigantic.

Finally, Mr. Zarcolnarcol raised his hand. He stood up and said to us all, "I think the red boat is attacking people in Lonely Lake because we need it to. We've made up this story about this horrible red boat driven by the devil. . . . "

"Or demons," Mr. Dordlenordle said.

"Or demons," Mr. Zarcolnarcol said. "And we have to have this legend or Lonely Lake would dry up and allow Walmart to come in here and put in that Supercenter they've been talking about for twenty-five years."

It was hard to tell when he sat down if there was agreement or not, because the entire lodge was silent for the first time in four hours.

He stood up again. "For example," he went on. "Has anyone seen any of the attacks?"

"I heard there was an attack yesterday at rocky pinion," someone said.

"I did too," someone added. "Some kid on a float board was cut all to ribbons. He looked like a pink slinky."

"And there was blood everywhere," someone else called out. "All the way to the old bridge."

People weren't standing and waiting to be identified now; they were just calling out.

"And it killed sixteen people in that church group of Goomberg," someone else called. "The red boat cut their houseboat in two and chewed them all up one by one."

"Presbyterians," someone said.

"The youth group," someone else added. "And part of the choir. I heard it was a retreat."

"Did you see it, any of the bodies or the ambulance?" Mr. Zarcolnarcol said.

"I heard they had trouble putting the bodies back together," someone said. "Legs and arms."

"It's the Devil's Boat!" Mr. Bakertaker said again, but now he almost screamed.

"There's no red boat," Mr. Zarcolnarcol said. "It's just Lonely Lake. It's always been Lonely Lake. Sometimes the wind blows from Forlorn Pass, and you can smell the pine forest there and in the evening if the clouds are low, the light turns pink reflected off Mount Lost and Lonely Lake glows too, the water so purple it seems like wine. And in the middle of the summer, like tonight, if you go to gold beach where the sandbar reaches out you can walk into the water so that your ankles tingle. Wade in. You will hear the steady motor of the cicadas. You will feel the memory of winter ice, and you will feel the melting snow of yesteryear, and the blood in your body will go down into your legs almost on a dare to feel the chill, the purple glowing chill of Lonely Lake."

We Went Up to Quencher's Point

We went up to Quencher's Point which was said to be haunted by a
suicide. You can park your car on the clay among the rough rocks as
big as houses overlooking Treachery where the gravel quarry has cut
the ragged escarpment. We'd gone up there at ten o'clock after the
state championship basketball game at Hatchcover and after we'd all
gone to Sidney's for the black forest shakes, and Jake and Mary Ellen
were in the front seat, and I was in the back with Dee Ann whom I
didn't know too well, but she was in Mrs. Eider's AP English with me
and liked Dylan Thomas and she had sat next to me at the basketball
game and then stood next to me at Sidney's Ice Cream and Cake and
poached a few spoonfuls of my shake and bumped my arm, like that.
I liked her and when we came onto Quencher's Point, she slid closer
to me so that I had to put my arm out around her. When we left the
dirt lane and turned onto the clay and drove among the neighborhood of boulders, it had gotten real quiet. The radio had been spitting
and cutting out, the AM station from Treachery which had a weak
signal. Its tower was never properly repaired after the tornado. They
found the topmost section speared into the boat dock at Drippers
Landing and they had trucked it back on a boat trailer, but they had
never put it back in place. That's going to be tricky work. Jake crept
his Oldsmobile among the towering rocks and nosed out onto the
overlook. He turned the radio off and then he leaned across Mary Ellen and rolled up that window; and Dee Ann leaned back to her side
and rolled up that window and then came back and snuggled under
my arm. It was a warm night, but not that warm, and so we sat with
the windows up and the four doors locked. Dee Ann was a beauty
in our school, without question, and I felt lucky and rich with the
few glowing minutes before our first kiss. She had big eyes, beautiful
eyes, and I could see that they were open, for my eyes were open. We

were full of ice cream and a little scared. I put my hand on her waist and felt the wonder of her stomach under the few folds of her summer dress. I could feel the bulb of her breast bumping the side of my thumb as we kissed. It was heavy and it floated.

It was three hundred feet. He jumped from one of the rocks into the quarry pit. He had a letter in his hand. He had a rose in his teeth. He'd taken off all of his clothes. It was a girl. She'd tucked a letter in her brassiere. She'd taken off her clothes. She cried out one word, a name, and that name haunts this place. He'd waved at a friend and then stepped backward into the air. She'd said something in a language that nobody even knew that she knew and then she jumped. He drank a fifth of Old Rigamarole whiskey and threw the bottle onto the rocks below before following it, and the bottle never broke. She knelt in prayer and then dived off the cliff. He was singing a song as he ran over the edge and he kept singing as he fell. Lots of people know which song, but never say. She said one word and it was *yes* and then threw her arms open and jumped. She was alone, and no one saw her leave the earth. She had been with her lover in his car and thought the distant lightning of a storm over Cloverboot was the light from her father's approaching car and she hurried, her dress in one hand, over the escarpment. He sat in his old Volkswagen and finished the last page of a book he was writing by hand with a ballpoint pen in a spiral notebook and then threw the pen over there or over there and leaped to his death and there are people who know where that book is but will never say. He had murdered the man found in the Beadtown orchard the month before. It was a mistake, but he could not stand the guilt. She'd had a baby at noon and left it on the post office steps in Crinshaw and she'd called the firechief there and told him and then she'd driven up here and run barefoot and purposeful over the cliff's edge. He had been turned down by Backerly College where he was going to study philosophy and astronomy and chemistry and geology, and the letter was in his vest pocket. She'd bumped her head in a bicycle accident a week before and had been strange for days, cackling and crying, laughing and humming, and calling her mother Ratuwary, which is the famous baking flour, and then one night she hitched a ride with a trucker and from the highway ran the rest of the way never stopping at the cliff's edge. No one ever located the trucker because he dropped into the Hissaloni River in a bridge accident that very week and no one will say his name. The boy and the girl jumped together on the count of three, but she hesitated and her nightgown caught on a scrub oak branch and they found her alive the next morning dangling there and shivering and she was sent to a girls' school in a city no one will name. Their parents forbid them to see each other, and they decided to jump and it was one-two-three, but the girl who was always funny jumped on two and when he saw her face just a few feet suddenly from him, but over the abyss, it made him unable to follow her and he never returned home and no one knows where he lives now, but two roses appear on her grave on every anniversary of her death. The boy and the girl were parking late at night after a basketball game years ago when even the schools had different names and at one point in the warm dark he felt the ghosts pass with a shiver like lifting linen, and her bare skin was an unworldly shock to his fingers, nothing this smooth ever was or walked the earth, and I opened my hand so that the mystery of Dee Ann's full breast fell into it perfectly, moist along the swollen bottom, and I wanted that feeling and the beating heart to be the one thing that I would know absolutely and forever. I wanted the warmth and the weight of her body printed in the stars and we kissed and now her eyes were closed and I lost where I was and she was and where we now began.

At night at Quencher's Point always after ten and before dawn, figures glide without a sound between the great boulders there, one and then another, shades of youth interrupting any view that the children in parked cars might have of the distant twinkling lights of the make-believe towns which lie on the planet below.

Teenagers Are Going Overnight to the Island without Supervision!

The teenagers were driving to the dock. Six teenagers were in the car talking and fooling around, laughing and being loud. They all talked at once, the three boys and the three girls, or they laughed. Tom was driving and singing a song, parts of a song he knew. Teri sat beside him waving her hands in the air to tell the story of Mr. Fudge, their history teacher. Jeff sat by the door pointing at the bits of the big lake they could see now that they were closer. Joyce sat behind him explaining what her mother had said about the weekend. Mary sat in the middle of the backseat, little Mary, her laugher sounded like a xylophone. Martin had his arm around her while he asked loud questions about what they had brought to drink.

The landing was empty and the old wooden dock stood in the purple lake. They could see the trees on the little island out on the horizon. They all were quiet, hauling their brown grocery bags full of celery and paper towels to the boat. They all knew that they were teenagers going overnight to the island without supervision. Tom sat so he could row the boat. He had driven the car and now he rowed the boat. He was Tom. They were quiet also for the moment that they launched into the lake, the oars creaking and each of the teenagers feeling the movement as Tom rowed.

"Has anyone been out here before?" Joyce asked. She had trailed her hand in the water, but now held it in her lap. Three big birds flew slowly over the boat. The shadows of the birds crossed over the teenagers. Slowly the six teenagers in the boat approached the island, and now they could see the pine trees at the water's edge. The teenagers looked at each other. There were six of them and so they each looked at the five others while the boat came into the small bay and Tom rowed until the boat hit sand.

They could see the little cabin in the clearing in the long shadows of the big trees. The teenagers climbed out of the boat: Terri, Joyce, Jeff, Tom, Martin, and then Mary. They lifted their sleeping bags and their grocery bags and walked single file though the tall grass toward the little log cabin.

"What did you bring?" Mary called.

"I brought paper towels and celery," Jeff said. He held up his celery and waved it in the evening light.

"We all brought paper towels and celery," Teri said.

"It's just one night," Tom said. "We can survive on celery and whiskey. Yes, I brought some whiskey."

"All right," Jeff said. "We can survive on that all right. I'm looking forward to drinking some whiskey on the island."

Then there was a sound that grew louder and louder, a noise like a scream only louder, a human cry that was so loud each of the teenagers lowered their heads. The wailing continued for a minute and then faded away into a sobbing gurgle.

"What was that noise?" Mary said.

"I don't know," Tom said. "Some noise. Come on."

The cabin was small and dark. Tom clomped up onto the porch and pushed open the front door. "Be careful where you step," he said. "The floor is rotting, but it will be all right."

One by one the teenagers watched their footsteps and entered into the dark little log cabin. There was nothing in the cabin but a crude wooden table. Each of the teenagers put their grocery bags on the table, six bags. The fireplace was made of round stones.

"We'll have to sleep on the floor."

"The sleeping bags zip together," Jeff said.

"We all know that," Joyce said.

The teenagers all threw their sleeping bags into a corner: Tom and Teri in one, Jeff and Joyce in one, and Martin and Mary in one.

"Have you ever seen so many paper towels?" Joyce said. "Someone should spill something."

"Don't spill the whiskey," Tom said. He cracked the lid from the whiskey bottle and drank from the bottle. It was so big it had a handle. "Well, we made it to the island," he said.

And he passed the bottle to Martin who said, "We made it to the island," and he took a drink. They all took a drink of whiskey from the bottle.

"This is the life," Teri said, "drinking whiskey on the island."

"Are we all going to sleep in the same room?" Mary said.

"Unless you want to sleep out in the woods," Martin said.

They could hear the wind in the trees. "It will be dark soon," Jeff said. "We should gather some firewood."

Outside, the teenagers felt the cold wind, and the trees loomed above them. They stayed close to the old cabin and gathered dead branches and armloads of wood. As they worked, picking up branches, the teenagers could hear voices crying in the island forest, and it sounded like children crying and old people and someone saying *boohoo boohoo* in sobs. Every time one of the teenagers would pick up a broken stick, he or she would stand and look into the forest from where the voices called in pain and anguish.

"What is that noise?" Joyce said.

"Nothing," Martin said. "It's the island."

"Did you know it would be like this?"

"No," he said, "You can never know about an island."

They gathered their sticks and walked quickly back and put the firewood on the porch of the old cabin.

"I'll build a fire," Tom said. He had driven the car, and rowed the boat, and opened the whiskey and now he showed everyone his matches. They were glad to see the matches. He broke a pile of sticks and put them in the fireplace. "Here," Jeff said. "Use some paper towel to start the fire." Tom knelt with the wad of paper and started the fire, a little yellow spot in the dark room.

"Who built this cabin?"

"I don't know," Tom said. "No one does."

"It was a guy who was murdered with his own axe," said Martin.

"I know," said Mary. "I can feel it."

"No way," Joyce said.

"Clunk," Martin said. "Right in the head with the axe. Right in this room." The six teenagers looked around the room.

"Who did it?" Joyce said.

Tom opened the whiskey bottle again and drank. He handed the bottle to each of the teenagers and they all drank.

"Who wants some celery?" Teri said.

"Let's all have some," Mary said. "With our whiskey."

"Have you ever seen so much celery?" Teri added.

Suddenly they heard a thumping on the front door.

"What is that?" Jeff said.

The thumping was regular, like *knock knock knock.*

"It's him," Joyce said. "He's back to see who's trespassing in the place where he was killed."

"Oh my god," Mary said.

"Listen," Martin whispered.

They heard the thumping go from one end of the porch to the other end of the porch.

"Do you want me to go out there and see who it is?" Tom said. "I will. I will go out there."

"No," Teri said. "Just stay here. There are six of us."

"It was probably just the wind knocking the firewood," Jeff said. "It probably wasn't the murdered man."

The teenagers were very quiet for a while and then they sat and ate celery which made crunching sounds. They ate celery and drank the rest of the whiskey, the big glass bottle traveling around and around the room until it was empty.

"Celery is good with whiskey," Teri said.

"And vice versa," said Tom

"This is some trip," Jeff said. "This is the life."

"We've got it made," Tom said.

Mary and Martin zipped their sleeping bags together and had crawled in. The fire had dwindled but there was still a glow in the room. Tom and Teri climbed into their sleeping bag, and Jeff and Joyce climbed into their sleeping bag.

"Goodnight everybody," Mary said. Everyone said goodnight.

They heard another sound now above the little crackling of the fire. It was a *drip drip drip.*

"What is that? Joyce said.

Tom sat up and looked at the floor by the table. "It's blood dripping from the ceiling."

"Oh," Joyce said. She got up and went to the table. "I don't want it to get on the celery or paper towels."

"Say," Mary said to Joyce. "Throw me my paper towels. I'm going to use it as a pillow."

Me too and me too, the other teenagers said.

They slept that way, the teenagers on the island, zipped in their sleeping bags with paper towels for pillows.

Biographical Note

Ron Carlson is the author of five story collections and six novels, including *Return to Oakpine* and *The Signal*. His fiction has appeared in *Harper's*, *The New Yorker*, *Playboy*, *GQ*, *Best American Short Stories*, and *The O. Henry Prize Stories*. His book of poems, *Room Service: Poems, Meditations, Outcries, & Remarks*, was published by Red Hen Press in 2012. His book on writing, *Ron Carlson Writes a Story*, is taught widely. He is the director of the writing program at the University of California at Irvine and lives in Huntington Beach, California.